THE WORLD OF UNDERGROUND GOLD MINING

Colouring & Activity Book

By

A H Iles

Disclaimer:

This is a work of fiction. Names, characters, businesses, places, events, locales, and incidents are either the products of the author's imagination or used in a fictitious manner. Any resemblance to actual persons, living or dead, or actual events is purely coincidental.

This book belongs to:

Get ready young mining explorer

You are about to embark on a fun colouring adventure so grab your crayons or pencils and let's explore the world of underground gold mining.

TAGBOARD

CHANGE TO CHANNEL 01 HAVE YOU TAGGED ON?

PARROT DECLINE
Mine Entrance

SAFETY FIRST!

Before you begin your exciting gold mining exploration and colouring, please:

- Use crayons or coloured pencils.
- Always ask an adult for help if you need it.
- Don't put colouring pens in your mouth.
- Clean up after you have finished colouring to keep your space safe and tidy.
- Wash your hands after you've finished colouring.

What You Will Learn

What Gold Mining Is

You will discover how gold is formed and mined from underground.

Roles of Miners

You will meet many mining characters and learn about their jobs.

Mining Equipment

You will learn about different machines and how they help get the gold out.

Safety in Mining

You will learn about safety as miners work together to keep everyone safe underground.

GOLD MINING WORDS YOU WILL LEARN

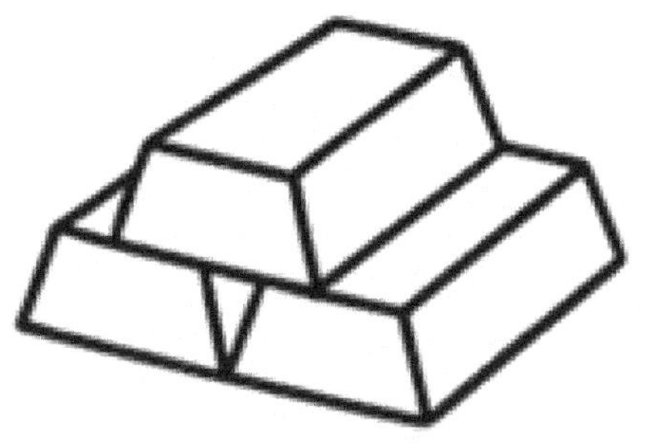

GOLD BARS

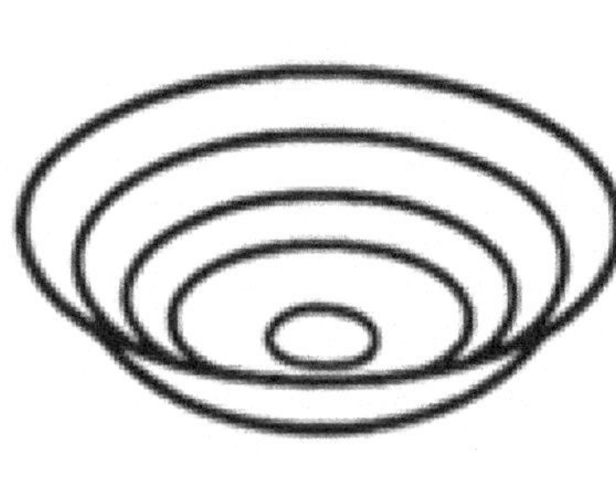

GOLD PAN

METAL DETECTOR

PERSONAL PROTECTIVE EQUIPMENT

GOLD ORE

DRILL

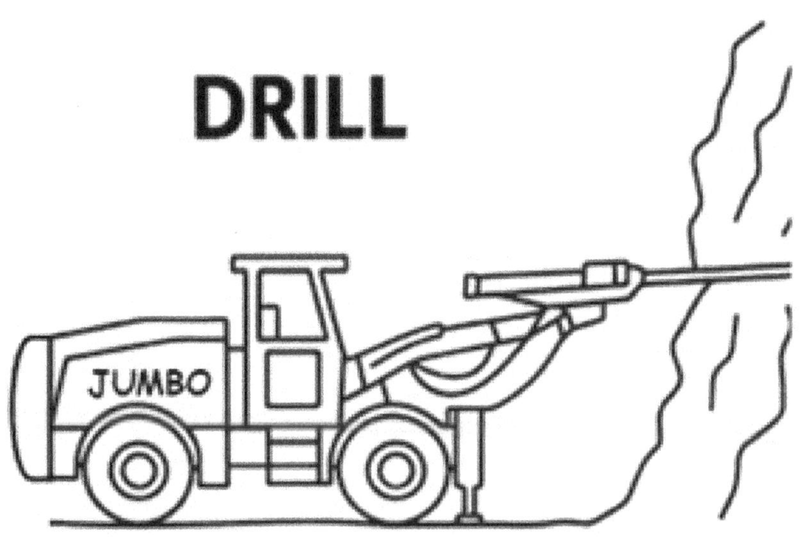

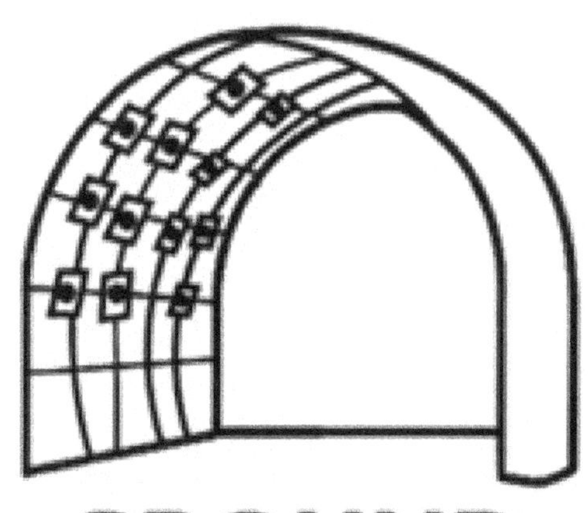

GROUND SUPPORT

WHAT IS GOLD AND HOW IS IT CREATED?

Gold is a shiny yellow metal that is rare and very valuable. People have used it for thousands of years.

A long time ago, gold came from space on huge rocks called Asteroids that crashed into Earth.

Over time Gold is transported by liquids such as water, and by volcanic systems, through cracks in the ground where it forms Gold deposits, also known as Gold ore. These gold deposits are what we mine today!

Gold deposits are then found by mining geologists by studying rock formations, using maps and exploration drilling machines.

A mine is then built to bring the gold ore out of the ground.

How is gold taken out of the ground and made in to a Gold Bar?

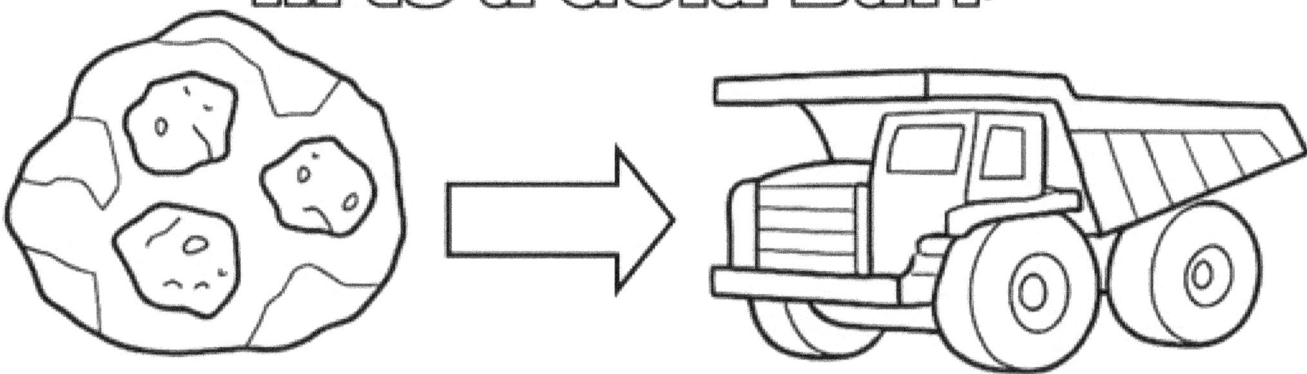

1. Finding the Gold in the rock.

2. Haul it to the gold mill where it is crushed.

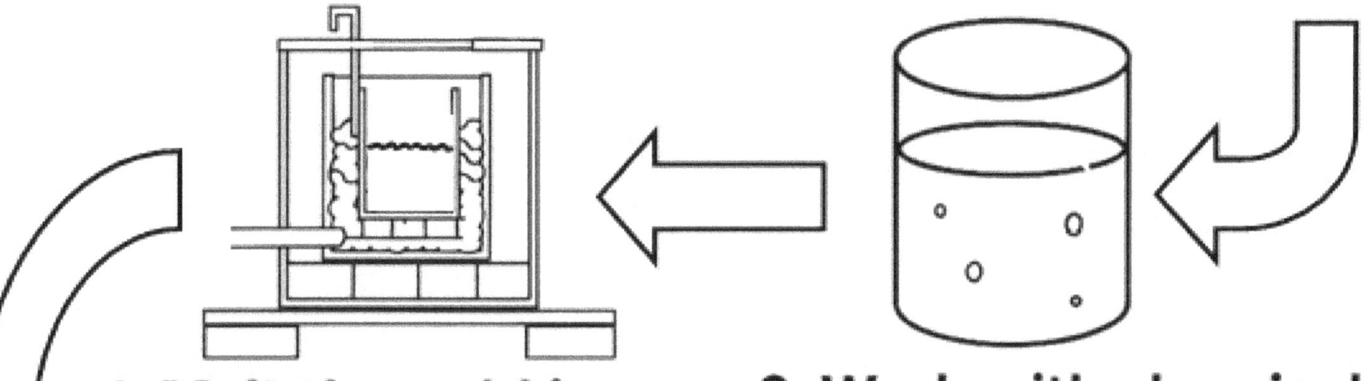

4. Melt the gold in a special furnace.

3. Wash with chemicals to separate the Gold from the rock.

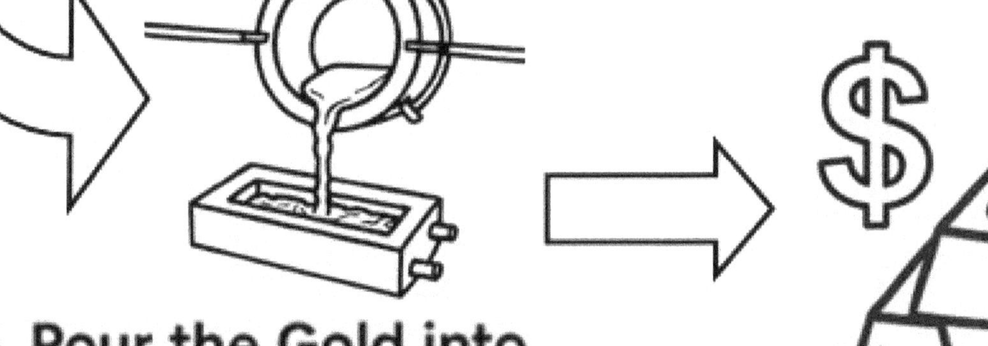

5. Pour the Gold into a mould which cools down and turns into a gold bar.

What does an underground gold mine look like?

BEFORE WE GO UNDERGROUND

We must put on our safety equipment (P.P.E.) for protection

LET'S MEET
THE CREW!

JERRY THE JUMBO OPERATOR

Jerry uses a big drill called a Jumbo to make holes in the rock underground which are used for blasting to find gold. Jerry drills holes in a pattern and make sure the drill goes in the right direction.

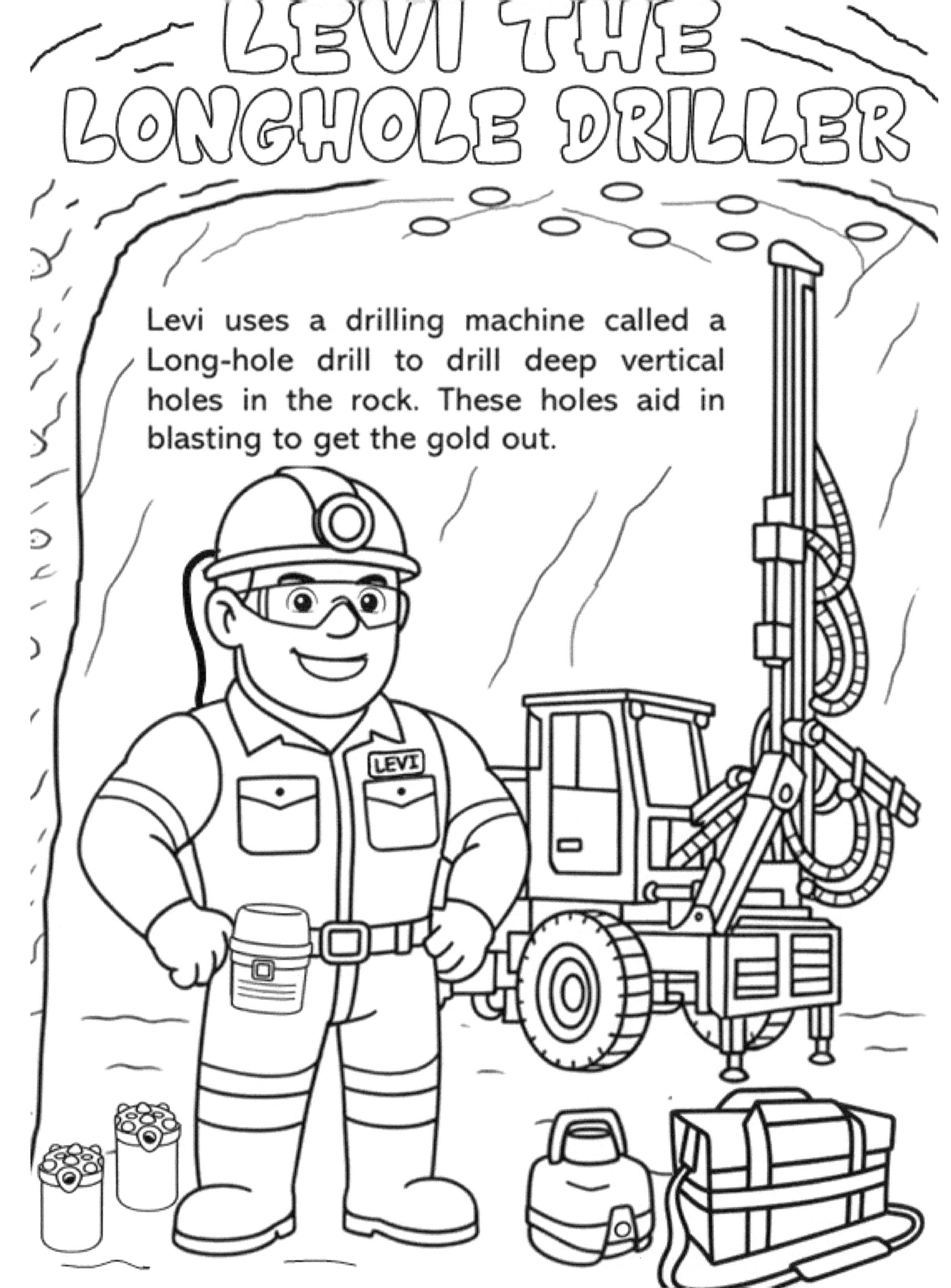

LEVI THE LONGHOLE DRILLER
Levi uses a drilling machine called a Long-hole drill to drill deep vertical holes in the rock. These holes aid in blasting to get the gold out.
LEVI

ARCHIE THE AIRLEG MINER

Archie uses a special handheld drill called an Airleg to make holes in the rock in tight spaces for blasting and digging.

The operator needs to be strong and steady to use the airleg.

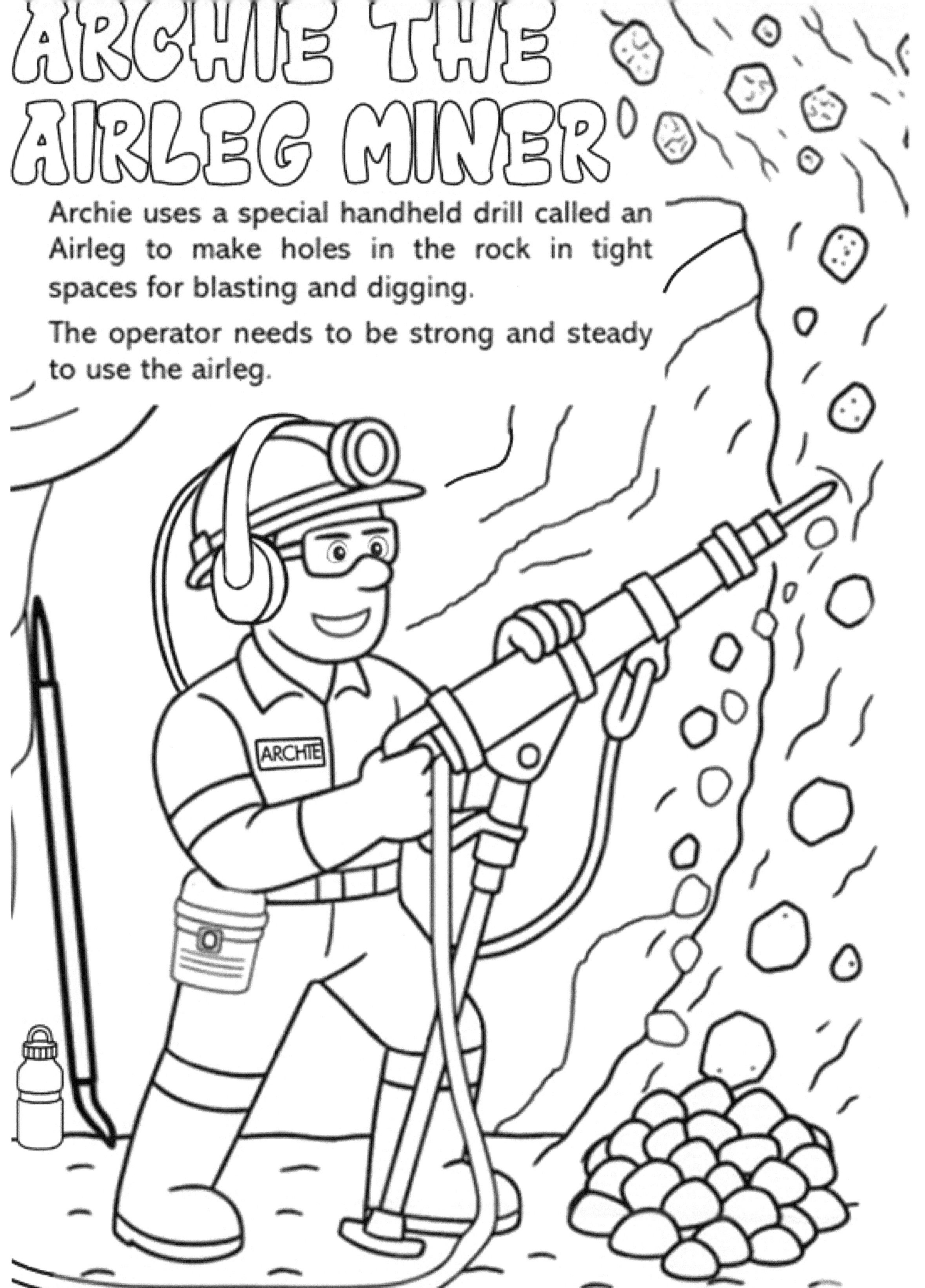

GEORGE THE GEOLOGIST

George is like a rock detective. He finds out where gold is underground, takes rock samples, makes maps and helps miners dig in the right place.

SUZI THE SURVEYOR

Suzi measures and maps the tunnels underground. She uses special tools like lasers and computers to make maps that help miners know where to dig safely and find the gold.

NOAH THE NIPPER

Noah is a helper who carries tools, supplies, and equipment to the work site and works closely with Jumbo Operators like Joe. Noah helps set up, clean the work area ,and needs to be strong and fit.

CODY THE CHARGE UP OPERATOR

Cody is in charge of handling and managing explosives in the mine. He puts the explosives into the holes that the drillers make, and then presses a button which explodes the rock. Cody must make sure he does his job safely.

LENNY THE LOADER OPERATOR
LENN
Lenny operates a Loader, often called a Bogger, to scoop up all the rocks that have been blasted and loads them onto an underground truck Sometimes he uses a remote control.

TESS THE TRUCK OPERATOR
Tess drives the big truck through twisty tunnels deep underground and dumps it on the surface to be turned into gold.
TESS

GROUND SUPPORT

Miners make tunnels safe so rocks don't fall.

They use **rock bolts, wire mesh,** and **shotcrete** (sprayed concrete) to hold the walls and roof, like glue and nets for the rock. Rock bolts are like giant nails that hold the mine together.

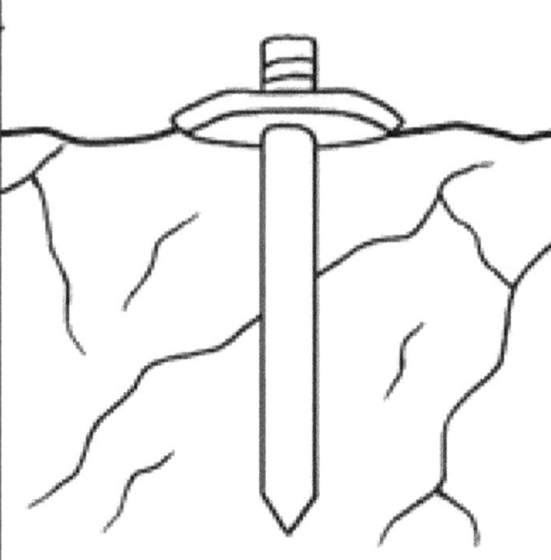

Split Sets

A long tube bolt that squeezes into the rock to hold it tight.

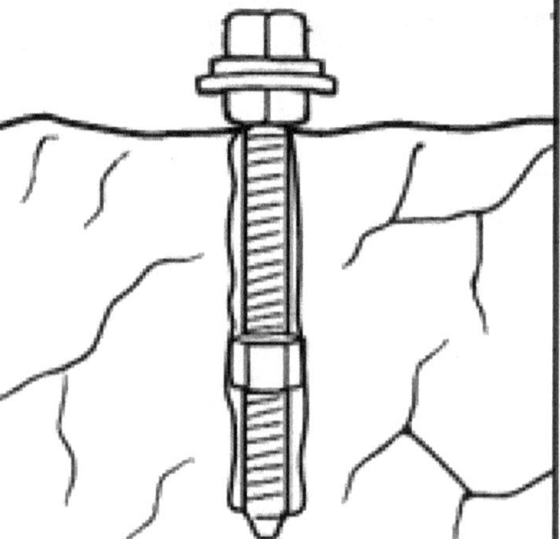

Chemical Bolts

A bolt glued into the rock with strong chemicals

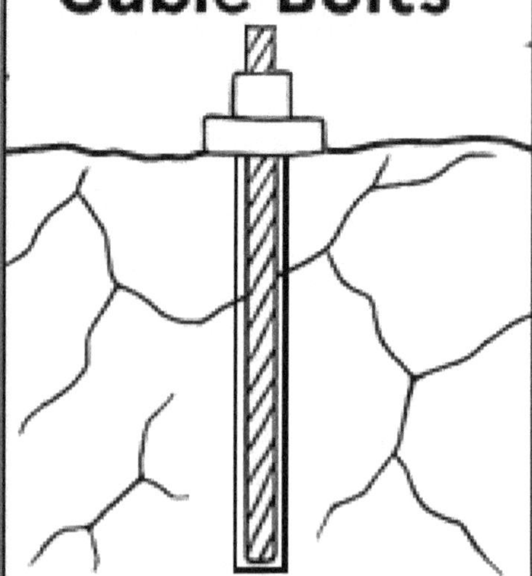

Cable Bolts

A long strong cable bolt filled with concrete

SARAH
THE SHOTCRETER
Sarah sprays special concrete on the walls and roof of the tunnels to stop rocks from falling to keep the mine safe.
SARAH
CEMENT
CEMENT
Dust Masks

GUS THE GRADER OPERATOR

Gus drives a big grader that smooths the bumpy roads so trucks and other vehicles can drive safely underground.

WILBUR
THE WATER TRUCK
OPERATOR
Wilbur drives a big water truck underground and sprays water on the roads to stop dust and keep the mine clean and safe.
WILBUR

ANGUS
THE AGI DRIVER
Angus drives a big concrete mixing truck underground. It's like a giant cake mixer on wheels! The truck mixes concrete as it moves though the tunnels and delivers it to the miners such as the Shotcreter.
ANGUS
EYE WASH STATION

SAMANTHA THE SERVICE CREW PERSON

Samantha helps keep the mine working by installing and maintaining air, water and ventilation.

STEVE THE SHIFTBOSS

Steve makes sure all the miners have jobs to do, checks everything is running smoothly, fixes problems and makes sure everyone is safe.

ERIC THE ELECTRICIAN
ERIC
Eric makes sure there is power for all the lights, phones, fans, radios and machines underground.

MACK
THE DIESEL MECHANIC

Mack fixes and looks after the big machines such as trucks, loaders and drilling machines. He makes sure all the drills and vehicles are working properly. If something breaks down Mack repairs it so the mine can keep running safely.

SPENCER THE STOREPERSON

Spencer looks after all the spare parts, tools and many other items that are needed to keep the mine running.

FRANK THE FOREPERSON

Frank manages all the activities underground
with the help of the Shiftboss

SIMONE THE SUPERINTENDENT

Simone manages key underground tasks, hires new underground miners and organizes equipment. She makes sure tasks are completed safely and on time with the help of Frank the foreperson.

EPHRAM THE ENGINEER

Ephram plans, designs, develops and manages the underground mining process.

SPIKE THE SAFETY OFFICER

Spike helps keep everyone protected at work by training the miners on the machines, teaching workplace safety and the rules of the mine.

Mike supervises and manages all underground mining projects, equipment, workforce, site rules, talks to other managers and makes sure everything complies with mining regulations and safety rules.

MINDY THE METALLURGIST

Mindy is like a metal scientist and works in the Gold Mill. She crushes, grids and extracts the gold from the rock so it can be turned into a gold bar.

WHAT IS GOLD USED FOR?

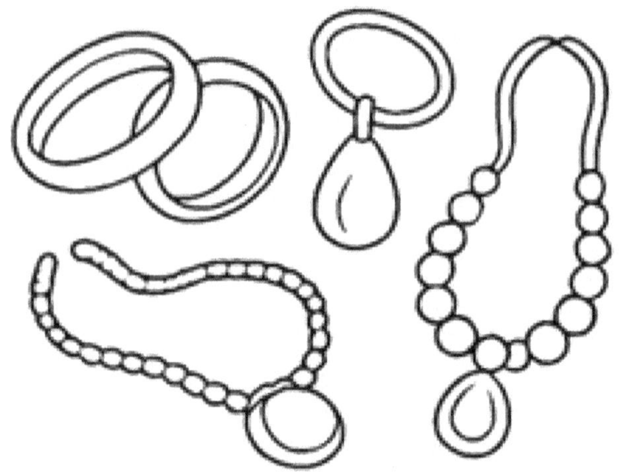

Rings, necklaces, bracelets, and earrings

Gold has been used as money for thousands of years!

Gold is used to make mobile phones, comuters, and televisions!

Gold is used to make art work such as vases and paintings.

Gold coating is used on astronaut helmets to protect them from solar radiation

Gold is used on trophies and medals to celebrate victories

YOU CAN FIND GOLD TOO! FINDING GOLD IS A FUN ADVENTURE!

Panning for Gold

Gold washes into small rivers and creeks – check riverbeds for sparkles! Fill a gold pan with dirt and water, shake it and swirl it around, and see if shiny gold stays at the bottom!

USING A METAL DETECTOR
Gold prospectors use special tools to help them look for gold like a metal detector to find gold just beneath the surface.

PROTECTING THE ENVIRONMENT

Our Earth is home to animals, plants, waterways and people. We must take care of it! The mine always protects them all by keeping the air and water clean, protects wildlife, and plants new trees and grass, a process called 'Revegetation'.

CONGRATULATIONS!
NOW THAT YOU HAVE EXPLORED
A MODERN UNDERGROUND
GOLD MINE, IT'S TIME FOR
ACTIVITIES
MINES RESCUE
FIRST AID

THE NUGGET MAZE
FIND THE GOLD NUGGETS
start here

Spot the Hazard!

Look carefully at the mine scene. Can you find all the eight hazards? Circle them and colour them in as you find them!

Cover answers before starting!

ANSWERS:

1. Liquid spill on the road.　2. Rocks on the road.　3. Rock about to fall from the ceiling.　4. Flat tyre on the truck.　5. Man not wearing a helmet.　6. Lady not wearing safety glasses　7. Broken wires hanging from the ceiling　8. Lady wearing thongs instead of safety boots.

MATCH THE MACHINE

Draw a line to match each underground machine with it's correct name and then colour them in.

1.

2.

3.

4.

5.

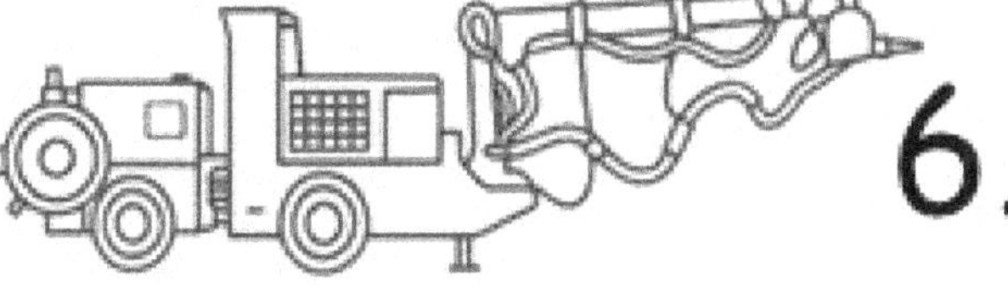

6.

7.

A. Agi Truck

B. Shotcreter

C. Loader

D. Jumbo

E. Water Truck

F. Longhole

G. Haul Truck

SPOT THE DIFFERENCES

Cover answers before starting!

ANSWERS:
1. Tree missing. 2. The man is not smiling. 3. Missing rod next to drilling machine.
4. Code is different on core tray. 5. Truck missing. 6. Plant missing.
7. Shirt pocket missing. 8. There are clouds. 9. Missing bird. 10. Cloud missing

Gold Mine Word Search!

Find the hidden mining words in the puzzle below! Circle each one as you find it. They can go up, down, across, or diagonal. Can you find them all?

```
G O L D O N B M T Z V O S R J U M B O S
U R Z O P N X U A M E Z B W B Y L U H A
M E I L A C L M H T N H L U J O T O M F
B F M G X D S X G T I M S A J S T I Y E
O J U U C P E K M A P S B T Q C P C R T
O P I R J P S R W H G I L X R H Q I R Y
T V D K N E O U L Z L P A E X F M U Y M
S T W D T A V W R F U Y S X V O C T O S
D M D B Q P C C T V L E T F N K F C W R
N W H B V W L E L C O R E Y M S Q A I Z
S E D O C M Y I W S L Y G L J M Y W E X
W S H I F T R H D K B A I R L E G N M Y
I G K J W C I G Q E S B C G N Z P I P K
J Q M E N I P P E R I V F J E X Z W M I
X A I H I G S F V G X Z L D L C Q L O T
O G V E K E F E S I O M K A T F E V F E
I L F K V H I F T I E K R N C T L U B M
D V C O I E Y F A K U W R Y Q X L U X L
A O L J M Q T E D E L Y A F R S W O A E
R G M E T A L A O M Y C B J T W P H B H
```

HIDDEN MINING WORDS

ORE GOLD BOLT JUMBO SAFETY LOADER
GLOVES NIPPER CORE SHIFT HAUL RADIO
HELMET METAL GUMBOOTS ROCK
BLAST AIRLEG MAPS VENT FURNACE

COLOUR BY NUMBERS

Use the colouring numbers below to bring this picture to life!

GOODBYE
young mining explorer

We hope you enjoyed learning about modern underground gold mining.

CERTIFICATE OF COMPLETION
This is to certify that
has completed their journey of
a modern underground gold mine
CONGRATULATIONS, YOUNG EXPLORER!
You've learned about hardworking miners, their amazing machines, and how they uncover gold deep underground and keep each other safe.
You are now an official
Underground Gold Mining Mate!
Signed,
The Undergound Gold Mining Team